Gingerbread Mouse

written and illustrated by Katy Bratun

HarperCollins*Publishers*

For my dad and mom, Rudy and Alma,
who made our Christmas wishes come true
−K.B.

Gingerbread Mouse
Copyright © 2008 by Katy Bratun
Manufactured in China. All rights reserved.
www.harperchildrens.com

Library of Congress Cataloging-in-Publication Data
Bratun, Katy.
    Gingerbread mouse / written and illustrated by Katy Bratun.
        p.   cm.
    Summary: An accident sends Mouse in search of a new home
at Christmas time and she finds what seems to be the perfect one
inside of a much larger house, but she meets a new friend with a
better idea.
    ISBN 0-06-009080-4 – ISBN 0-06-009081-2 (lib. bdg.)
    [1. Mice–Fiction.   2. Dwellings–Fiction.   3. Santa Claus–Fiction.
4. Christmas–Fiction.]   I. Title.
PZ7.B787785 Gi   2008   2002151602
[E]–dc21   CIP
                                                                  AC

Typography by Elynn Cohen
1 2 3 4 5 6 7 8 9 10
❖
First Edition

Gingerbread Mouse

A winter snow had covered the forest, but Mouse was cozy in her tiny home. She was snuggled under the covers fast asleep.

CRACK! Mouse woke up and ran outside.
What was that sound? A huge branch
crashed to the ground, missing her by
inches. "Oh, no!" Mouse cried. Her cozy
home was ruined!

Climbing a tall tree, Mouse saw the twinkling lights of a house nearby. "I will look for a new home there," she said.

After a long, cold journey, she reached the big house. A warm light glowed from the window. She climbed up to take a peek. Mouse couldn't believe her eyes! There, inside the house, was her new home, just her size—almost like magic. But how could she get in?

Then Mouse saw her chance. She jumped up onto the tree as it brushed by and was inside the house in a twinkling.

Mouse scurried up onto the table.
She couldn't wait to move in!

She made a small
box into a dresser.

She made a rug and
curtains from ribbon
and string.

She made a rocking chair from cardboard.

"This is starting to feel like home,"
she said softly as she dropped off to sleep.

Suddenly there was a huge crash! Mouse
jumped up from her bed. "Ouch!" she heard
someone say. A giant man in a red suit
stumbled into the room from the fireplace,
rubbing his head. He pulled packages from a
large bag and placed them under the tree.

"You have a nice little home," he said as he filled the stockings over the fireplace.

"You mean ME?" Mouse asked.

"You might need a place that will last a bit longer, though," he said as he sipped his cocoa. "Maybe I can help." He stood up and brushed cookie crumbs from his coat. Then he pulled one last gift from his bag.

Mouse gasped in surprise. There in front of her was the nicest gift she could imagine! "It's beautiful!" she cried. But when she turned around, the man in the red suit was gone. "Ho! Ho! Ho!" she heard echoing from the chimney.

Mouse settled in right away.

On Christmas morning, the snow was falling softly outside the window. Mouse got up bright and early to watch the presents being opened.

Later Christmas night, Mouse sat happily knitting a sweater in her new home. She heard a soft knocking sound. She peeked out the door and saw a package on the doorstep. A small card was attached with ribbon.